# BUNCHES OF PASSION

## COZY AUTUMN ROMANCE

### ANN LAUREL

Truth is stranger than fiction, but it is because Fiction is obliged to stick to possibilities; Truth isn't.

— MARK TWAIN

# CHAPTER ONE

*Q*uinn

I took a deep breath, inhaling the crisp autumn air mingled with the scent of caramel apples and cinnamon. The Doveport Harvest Moon Festival was in full swing, and here I was, standing behind my rickety booth, watching him approach. Bennet Winslow, the handsome winemaker from the local vineyard, his dark hair tousled by the evening breeze, was heading straight for me with a smile that could melt the first frost.

"Looks like you could use a hand," he said, eyeing my precarious tower of brochures threatening to topple over.

I brushed a strand of auburn hair from my face, hoping he didn't notice the blush creeping up my cheeks. "Is it that obvious?" I laughed, trying to sound more confident than I felt. Inside, my stomach was doing somersaults. This was not how I'd envisioned my big debut at the festival going.

As we worked together to arrange my booth, I couldn't help but steal glances at him. His firm hands, calloused from working in the vineyard, moved with surprising grace as he helped me set up my event planning displays. The warm light from the string of Edison bulbs overhead cast a golden glow on his features, making him look like he'd stepped right out of a harvest-themed romance novel.

"So, Quinn Hartley Events, huh?" he said, reading my banner. "You're new in town, aren't you?"

I nodded, my stomach doing a little flip at the way he said my name. "Moved here a few months ago. Trying to make a name for myself in the event planning world." I gestured to the modest display of autumn-themed center-pieces and event proposals. "Though I'm starting to think I bit off more than I could chew with this festival booth."

"Well, you've certainly picked the right season," Bennet grinned, gesturing at the surrounding festival. "Doveport loves its autumn celebrations. And from what I can see, you've got a knack for capturing that fall magic."

His compliment warmed me more than the oversized sweater I was wearing. "Thanks," I said, fiddling with a small pumpkin on the display. "I've always loved autumn. There's something so... I don't know, magical about it. The colors, the scents, the way everything feels both ending and beginning at the same time."

Bennet's eyes lit up. "I know exactly what you mean. It's like that moment when you first taste a new wine, there's a hint of what's passed, but also the promise of something new and exciting."

As the evening wore on, Bennet stayed by my booth, chatting with me between visitors. We swapped stories about our favorite fall traditions, and I opened up about my struggles to establish my business.

"It's just been harder than I expected," I admitted, arranging a bouquet of silk maple leaves for the hundredth time. "I left a steady job in the city to pursue this dream, and some days I wonder if I made a huge mistake."

Bennet leaned against the booth, his brow furrowed in

thought. "Starting something new is always a risk," he said. "But from what I've seen tonight, you've got talent. And passion. That counts for a lot."

I smiled, touched by his encouragement. "Thanks. I just wish the rest of Doveport saw it that way. So far, I've had more people asking me for directions to the apple bobbing station than inquiring about my services."

He chuckled, the sound warm. "Give it time. Doveport can be slow to embrace newcomers, but once they do, you're family."

As if on cue, a group of festival-goers approached, their eyes lighting up at the sight of Bennet.

"There's our favorite winemaker!" an older woman exclaimed. "We were hoping to catch you. When's the next tasting at the vineyard?"

I watched as Bennet effortlessly charmed the group, discussing wine varieties and upcoming events at the winery. He had a way of making everyone feel like they were the most important person in the conversation. It was impressive, to say the least.

When the group moved on, promising to stop by the winery soon, Bennet turned back to me with an apologetic smile. "Sorry about that. Occupational hazard of being the local wine guy."

I waved off his apology. "Are you kidding? That was amazing. You really know how to work a crowd."

He shrugged modestly. "It's easy when you love what you do. Speaking of which," he paused, a thoughtful look in his warm brown eyes, "the winery hosts a lot of events. Maybe we could collaborate sometime."

My heart skipped a beat at the suggestion, but a nagging voice in the back of my mind reminded me of past disappointments. I had experienced being burned before, trusting too easily in business partnerships that had left me scrambling to pick up the pieces.

"That's a generous offer," I said cautiously, "but I'm not sure I'm ready for collaborations just yet. I'm still trying to find my footing here."

Bennet nodded, understanding in his eyes. "No pressure. But if you ever want to brainstorm ideas over a glass of wine, you know where to find me."

As the festival wound down, the crowd thinned out, leaving pockets of laughter and the soft glow of lanterns in its wake. Bennet helped me pack up my booth, our hands brushing as we folded my tablecloth. The contact sent a shiver down my spine that had nothing to do with the cool night air.

"Thanks for your help," I said, suddenly shy. "I don't know how I would have managed without you."

"It was my pleasure," he replied, his smile warm and genuine. "Will I see you at the autumn craft fair next week?"

I hesitated for a moment, then nodded. "I'll be there. Someone's got to show this town how to throw a proper fall-themed party."

Bennet laughed, the sound rich and inviting. "I'm looking forward to it already."

As I watched him walk away, blending into the crowd of festival-goers, I couldn't shake the feeling that something had shifted. For the first time since moving to Doveport, I felt a spark of excitement about what the future might hold.

I may have come to the Harvest Moon Festival to promote my business, but I left with something far more valuable with the possibility of a new beginning, as crisp as the autumn air around me.

The next morning, I woke to the sound of rain

pattering against the window of my small apartment above Doveport's only bookstore. The scent of brewing coffee and the faint mustiness of old books from the shop below filled the cozy space. I stretched, my muscles aching from the previous night's booth setup, and padded over to the window.

The town looked different in the soft, grey light of a rainy day. The colorful banners and decorations from the festival hung limp and sodden, but there was a certain charm to it all. It reminded me of why I'd chosen Doveport in the first place, with the perfect blend of quaint and quirky that seemed tailor-made for memorable events.

As I sipped my coffee, my mind wandered back to Bennet and his offer of collaboration. Part of me, the part that still stung from past betrayals, wanted to dismiss it outright. But another part, the part that his sweet smile and genuine interest in my work had captivated, couldn't stop turning over the possibilities.

I grabbed my ever-present notebook and started jotting down ideas. A wine-tasting event with perfectly paired seasonal hors d'oeuvres. A harvest-themed wedding showcase at the vineyard. A *Sip and Paint* night featuring autumnal landscapes.

Before I knew it, I'd filled three pages with scribbled concepts. I stared at them, a mix of excitement and trepidation bubbling in my chest. This was exactly why I'd started Quinn Hartley Events, to bring these kinds of magical moments to life. But could I really trust someone I'd just met with my fledgling business?

The day passed in a blur of follow-up emails to potential clients from the festival and planning for the upcoming craft fair. By late afternoon, the rain had cleared, leaving behind that peculiar golden light that only seems to exist in autumn. On a whim, I took a walk through town, hoping the fresh air would clear my head.

Doveport was picture-perfect in the post-rain glow. The maple trees lining Main Street were just beginning to turn, their leaves a patchwork of green, gold, and crimson. I passed by quaint storefronts decorated for fall, their windows filled with pumpkins, scarecrows, and cozy sweaters.

As I rounded the corner onto Elm Street, I nearly collided with someone coming out of the local coffee shop, The Percolator.

"Oh! I'm so sorry, I wasn't watching where I was..." I trailed off as I realized who it was. "Bennet?"

He grinned, steadying the two coffee cups in his hands. "Quinn! Just the person I was hoping to run into. Though maybe not quite so literally."

I laughed, feeling that now-familiar flutter in my stomach. "Sorry about that. I was lost in thought."

"No harm done," he said, then held out one cup. "I don't suppose you'd like a pumpkin spice latte? I ordered an extra by mistake."

I hesitated for a moment before taking the cup. "That's really sweet of you, but I should probably mention, I'm actually allergic to pumpkin. Ironic, I know, given my love for all things autumn."

Bennet's eyes widened in surprise, then crinkled with amusement. "Well, that certainly puts a twist on things. How about we trade? This one's just a regular vanilla latte."

As we swapped cups, our fingers brushed again, and a twinge of excited energy flowed up my arm. We fell into step together, strolling down the leaf-strewn sidewalk.

"So, how are you feeling about the festival?" Bennet asked, taking a sip of his latte. "Get any promising leads?"

I sighed, the weight of my struggles to settle back on

my shoulders. "A few nibbles, but nothing concrete yet. I'm starting to wonder if I made a mistake, trying to break into such a tight-knit community."

Bennet was quiet for a moment, his brow furrowed in thought. "You know," he said finally, "when I first took over the winery from my grandparents, I felt the same way. Everyone knew the Winslow name, but they weren't sure about this new kid with his fancy degree and big ideas."

I looked at him in surprise. "Really? But you seem so established. Like you've always belonged here."

He chuckled, shaking his head. "Trust me, it took time. And a lot of trial and error. But you know what made the difference?"

"What?"

"I stopped trying to be what I thought Doveport wanted, and started showing them who I really was. Once people saw my genuine passion for winemaking and for this town, things started to click."

We had reached the small park at the center of town, its wrought-iron benches surrounded by beds of chrysanthemums and ornamental cabbages. Bennet gestured to the bench, and we sat down.

"Quinn," he said, turning to face me, "I meant what I said last night. I think you've got something special. Your ideas, your enthusiasm is exactly what this town needs. You just need to give people a chance to see it."

A lump formed in my throat, touched by his words. "Thanks, Bennet. That means a lot, coming from you."

He smiled, and for a moment, I found myself lost in the warmth of his brown eyes. Then, clearing his throat, he reached into his jacket pocket and pulled out a small, folded piece of paper.

"I, uh, actually had an idea I wanted to run by you," he

said, suddenly looking nervous. "It's just a rough concept, but I thought maybe..."

As he unfolded the paper, I glimpsed what looked like a sketch of the vineyard, with notes scribbled in the margins. My curiosity piqued, I leaned in closer.

"So, every year, the winery hosts a harvest dinner," Bennet explained, pointing to different parts of the sketch. "It's usually pretty standard with good food, good wine, but nothing too exciting. I was thinking, what if we turned it into something more experiential?"

I nodded, encouraging him to continue.

"Picture this," he said, his eyes lighting up with enthusiasm. "Guests arrive at sunset, greeted with a glass of our seasonal sparkling apple wine. They take a twilight tour of the vineyard, learning about the harvest process. Then, dinner is served at long tables set up between the vines, with each course paired perfectly with one of our wines."

As he spoke, I could see it all unfolding in my mind's eye with the soft glow of lanterns, the rustic elegance of the table settings, the way the fading sunlight would paint the vineyard in shades of gold and purple.

"And here's where I thought you might come in," Bennet continued, his voice a mix of excitement and uncertainty. "The décor, the overall flow of the evening, maybe even some kind of interactive element for the guests. I have a feeling you'd knock it out of the park."

I stared at him, my mind racing with possibilities. It was exactly the event I'd dreamed of planning when I started my business. But the nagging voice of doubt was still there, whispering warnings about getting in too deep, too fast.

Bennet sensed my hesitation. "Look, I know we just met, and I completely understand if you're not comfortable jumping into a partnership. But even if you just want to consult, give some advice. I'd be grateful for your input."

I took a deep breath, feeling like I was standing on the edge of a cliff. On one side was the safety of sticking to my solo path, protecting myself from potential disappointment. On the other was the exhilarating possibility of creating something truly magical, of finally making my mark on Doveport.

"Can I think about it?" I asked, my voice barely above a whisper.

Bennet nodded, his smile understanding. "Of course. Take all the time you need." He stood up, brushing a few stray leaves from his jeans. "I should get back to the winery. But Quinn?"

I looked up at him, struck again by how the autumn light seemed to soften his features, making him look almost ethereal.

"Whatever you decide, I meant what I said before. You've got something special. Don't let fear hold you back from sharing it with the world."

As I watched him walk away, his words echoed in my mind. Don't let fear hold you back. Wasn't that exactly why I'd left my safe, predictable job in the city? Why I'd chosen Doveport, of all places, to start my business?

I pulled out my notebook, flipping to a blank page. At the top, I wrote "Winslow Vineyard Harvest Dinner" and underlined it twice. Then, almost without conscious thought, I began to sketch and scribble, ideas flowing faster than I could get them down on paper.

As the sun dipped below the horizon, painting the sky in brilliant shades of orange and pink, I realized I'd filled nearly ten pages with ideas. My hand was cramping, and my latte had gone cold, but I felt more alive than I had in months.

I stood up, clutching my notebook to my chest like a precious treasure. I didn't know exactly what the future held, or if I was ready to take this leap with Bennet. But for the first time since moving to Doveport, I felt like I was exactly where I was meant to be.

As I walked home, the street lamps flickered to life around me. I just knew something big was just around the corner. Whether it was a professional breakthrough, a personal connection, or both, only time would tell..

## CHAPTER TWO

*B*ennet

The crisp September air nipped at my cheeks as I navigated through the bustling crowd at the Doveport Autumn Craft Fair. I carried boxes of wine samples in my arms, finding comfort in the familiar weight as I searched for Quinn's booth. The scent of cinnamon and apples wafted through the air, mingling with the earthy aroma of my Cabernet Franc.

I spotted her before she saw me, her auburn hair catching the morning light like burnished copper. She was struggling with a stubborn tent pole, her brow furrowed in concentration. I couldn't help but smile at the determined set of her jaw.

"Need a hand there, event planner extraordinaire?" I called out, setting down my boxes.

Quinn looked up, surprise and relief flooding her features. "Bennet! I didn't expect to see you here so early."

I grinned, already moving to help with the tent. "Well, I couldn't let Doveport's newest entrepreneur face the craft fair alone, could I?"

As we worked together to set up her booth, I was hyper-aware of every accidental brush of our hands, every shared laugh. Quinn had a way of making even the most mundane tasks feel like an adventure.

"So, what's the grand plan for today?" I asked, helping her arrange a display of autumn-themed centerpieces. "Going to wow the locals with your event planning prowess?"

Quinn laughed, the sound warming me more than any glass of mulled wine ever could. "That's the idea. Though I'm starting to think I should have gone with a more traditional approach. Doveport seems to like things, well, Doveport-y."

I raised an eyebrow, intrigued. "Doveport-y? Do tell."

She gestured to the surrounding booths, all decked out in typical harvest fair fashion. "You know, lots of gourds, hay bales, the occasional scarecrow. Don't get me wrong, it's charming. But I was hoping to bring something a little different to the table."

I looked at her booth, taking in the sleek, modern centerpieces and the elegant event portfolios. It was different, sure, but in the best possible way. "I think it's perfect," I said softly. "Doveport could use a little shaking up."

Quinn's eyes met mine, and for a moment, I forgot how to breathe. There was something in her gaze, a mix of vulnerability and determination, that made me want to move mountains for her.

The sound of the fair's opening bell broke the moment. Quinn jumped, nearly knocking over a vase of silk autumn leaves. "Oh god, it's starting. I'm not ready. I'm so not ready."

I caught her hand, giving it a reassuring squeeze. "Hey, you've got this. And I'll be right over there if you need anything, okay?"

She nodded, taking a deep breath. "Thanks, Bennet. I don't know what I'd do without you."

As I made my way to the Winslow Vineyard booth, I realized I was the lucky one here.

The morning flew by in a whirlwind of wine tastings and small talk. I constantly glanced over at Quinn's booth, watching as she charmed potential clients with her infectious enthusiasm. Every so often, our eyes would meet across the crowded fairground, and I'd feel that now-familiar flutter in my chest.

During a lull in visitors, I made my way back to her booth, two steaming cups in hand. "Thought you could use a pick-me-up," I said, offering her a cup of spiced cider. "Don't worry, it's pumpkin-free."

Quinn's face lit up as she took the cup. "My hero," she said, inhaling the fragrant steam. "How did you remember about the pumpkin allergy?"

I shrugged, trying to play it cool. "I pay attention to the important things."

We fell into a conversation, discussing the fair and upcoming autumn events. Quinn's ideas were a breath of fresh air, full of creativity and modern twists on classic traditions.

"You know," I said, an idea forming, "I'd love to show you around the vineyard sometime. Maybe it could spark some inspiration for that harvest dinner we talked about."

Quinn hesitated, and I could see the conflict in her eyes. "I don't know, Bennet. It's a tempting offer, but..."

"No pressure," I assured her quickly. "Just a friendly tour. And hey, if you come up with any brilliant event ideas while we're there, who am I to complain?"

She laughed, shaking her head. "You're persistent, I'll give you that. Alright, you've got yourself a deal. But just a tour, okay?"

I held up my hands in mock surrender. "Scout's honor. Just a tour."

As the fair wound down, I helped Quinn pack up her booth. The day had been a success for both of us, with plenty of interested clients and wine orders to show for it.

"So, about that tour," I said as we loaded the last box into her car. "Are you free tomorrow afternoon?"

Quinn bit her lip, considering. "I suppose I could squeeze it in. For research purposes, of course."

I grinned, already looking forward to it. "Of course. Purely professional."

The next day dawned bright and clear, a perfect autumn day that seemed almost too good to be true. I spent the morning in a flurry of activity, making sure everything at the vineyard was in top shape for Quinn's visit.

When she arrived, looking effortlessly beautiful in a rust-colored sweater and jeans, I had to remind myself to breathe. "Welcome to Winslow Vineyard," I said, gesturing to the rolling hills of grapevines behind me. "Ready for the grand tour?"

Quinn nodded, her eyes wide as she took in the scenery. "It's beautiful, Bennet. I had no idea it was so 9vast."

I chuckled, leading her down a path between the vines. "It's been in my family for generations. My grandfather planted some of these vines himself."

As we walked, I opened up about the vineyard's history, my journey into winemaking, and the challenges of balancing tradition with innovation. Quinn listened intently, asking thoughtful questions and offering insights I'd never considered.

We paused at the top of a hill, looking out over the vineyard. The afternoon sun bathed everything in a golden light, making the changing leaves look like they were on fire.

"It's breathtaking," Quinn murmured, her shoulder brushing against mine.

I turned to look at her, struck by the way the light played across her features. "Yeah," I said softly, "it really is."

Our eyes met, and for a moment, I thought about closing the distance between us. The air seemed charged with possibility.

But before I could make a move, a familiar voice called out from behind us. "Bennet! There you are, my boy!"

I turned to see my grandfather making his way up the hill, his weathered face creased in a smile. "And who's this lovely young lady?"

"Grandpa, this is Quinn Hartley," I said, trying to hide my disappointment at the interruption. "She's the new event planner in town I told you about."

My grandfather's eyes lit up with interest. "Ah, yes! The one with all the fresh ideas. It's a pleasure to meet you, my dear."

Quinn shook his hand, her professional demeanor sliding into place. "The pleasure's all mine, Mr. Winslow. Your grandson has been telling me all about the vineyard's rich history."

"Please, call me Oak," my grandfather insisted. "Any friend of Bennet's is family here." He turned to me, his expression growing serious. "Speaking of family, Bennet, we need to discuss the harvest schedule. There's a storm system moving in next week, and we may need to adjust our plans."

I nodded, feeling the weight of responsibility settle back onto my shoulders. "Of course, Grandpa. I'll be right there." I turned to Quinn, apology written all over my face. "I'm sorry, I need to..."

She waved off my concern with a smile. "Don't worry about it. Duty calls, right? I should be heading back anyway. Thank you for the tour, Bennet. It was... illuminating."

As I watched her walk back to her car, I couldn't shake the feeling that I was letting something important slip away. But the vineyard had been my family's lifeblood for generations. I couldn't just abandon my responsibilities, no matter how tempting the alternative might be.

"She seems like a lovely girl," my grandfather said, watching Quinn drive away. "Reminds me a bit of your grandmother, you know. That same spark in her eyes."

I smiled, remembering the stories of how my grandparents had met. "Yeah, she's something special alright."

Grandpa clapped me on the shoulder. "Just remember, my boy, there's more to life than just the vineyard. Your grandmother and I built this place together, side by side. Don't let fear hold you back from finding that kind of partnership."

His words echoed in my mind as we made our way back to the main house. I'd always seen my dedication to the vineyard as a strength, a way of honoring my family's legacy. But what if it was also holding me back from something equally important?

As we pored over weather reports and harvest schedules, I found my thoughts drifting back to Quinn. Her laugh, her creative ideas, the way she saw the world in vibrant possibilities. I realized with a start that I wanted her to be a part of this world, my world.

But how could I find a balance between my growing feelings for her and the responsibilities that had been instilled in me since childhood? The vineyard needed me, especially with the challenges of an early harvest looming. And yet, the thought of letting Quinn slip away made my chest ache in a way I'd never experienced before.

The vineyard turned shades of orange and purple as the

sun sank low in the west and I made a decision. I couldn't keep living with one foot in the past and one in the future. Something had to give.

I pulled out my phone, my finger hovering over Quinn's number. Taking a deep breath, I pressed call.

"Hello?" Her voice came through, tinged with surprise.

"Quinn, hey," I said, my heart racing. "I was wondering if you'd like to have dinner with me tomorrow night. There's something I'd like to discuss with you."

There was a pause on the other end, and for a moment, I feared I'd overstepped. But then I heard her soft laugh. "I'd love to, Bennet. What did you have in mind?"

I grinned, already planning something. "How about you let me surprise you? I promise it'll be an event worthy of Quinn Hartley Events."

# CHAPTER THREE

*Q*uinn

I stood in the middle of the vineyard, the setting sun painting the sky in shades of pink and gold, my hands sticky with grape juice and my heart racing with a mixture of excitement and nerves. Bennet stood just a few feet away, his dark hair tousled by the autumn breeze, a boyish grin on his face as he held up a cluster of plump purple grapes.

"Think fast, Quinn!" he called out, tossing the bunch in my direction.

I laughed, fumbling to catch it, the sweet aroma of ripe fruit filling the air. "You know, when you said you wanted to take me on a surprise date, I didn't expect manual labor to be involved," I teased, popping a grape into my mouth.

Bennet chuckled, moving closer. "Hey now, this is prime Winslow family bonding activity. Besides," he added, his voice dropping to a lower, more intimate tone, "I thought you might appreciate a hands-on experience of the vineyard."

A blush crept up my cheeks, and it wasn't just from the

exertion of grape picking. There was something about the way Bennet looked at me, like I was the most fascinating person he'd ever met, that made my stomach do somersaults.

"Well, I have to admit," I said, gesturing to the breathtaking view around us, "this beats any fancy restaurant. Though I'm not sure how I'm going to get all this grape juice out of my clothes."

Bennet's eyes twinkled mischievously. "I might have a solution for that. Come on, I want to show you something."

He took my hand, sending a jolt of electricity up my arm, and led me through the rows of grapevines. As we walked, I couldn't help but marvel at how natural it felt, being here with him like this. It was so different from the high-pressure, competitive world of event planning I was used to in the city.

We crested a small hill, and I gasped. Before us lay a picturesque clearing, overlooking the entire vineyard. They had set up a rustic wooden table in the picturesque clearing, complete with flickering candles, a spread of artisanal cheeses and fruits, and two gleaming wine glasses.

"Bennet," I breathed, taking it all in. "This is incredible."

He squeezed my hand gently. "I thought we could do a little wine tasting. And maybe clean up a bit," he added with a grin, nodding towards a small basin of water and some towels he'd thoughtfully set out.

As we washed the grape juice from our hands, I couldn't help but steal glances at Bennet. The fading sunlight caught the angles of his face, highlighting the strong line of his jaw and the warmth in his brown eyes. I'd been fighting my growing feelings for him, telling myself I needed to focus on my career, on making Quinn Hartley Events a success.

But in moments like these, it was getting harder and harder to remember why.

Once we settled at the table, Bennet poured two glasses of a pale golden wine. "This is our Autumn Harvest Chardonnay," he explained, his voice taking on that passionate tone he always got when talking about wine. "It's got notes of apple and pear, with just a hint of oak. I thought it would pair nicely with the Brie."

I took a sip, closing my eyes as the flavors danced across my tongue. "It's beautiful," I said, opening my eyes to find Bennet watching me intently. "You really have a gift for this, you know."

He smiled, with more vulnerability in his expression. "Thanks. It means a lot to hear you say that. Sometimes I wonder if I'm living up to my family's legacy, you know?"

I nodded, understanding all too well the pressure of trying to prove yourself. "I get that. But Bennet, from what I've seen, you're not just living up to their legacy. You're building on it, making it your own."

He reached across the table, his fingers brushing mine. "You know, that's what I admire about you, Quinn. You're not afraid to take risks, to try something new. Your ideas for events, they're so fresh and exciting. This town needs someone like you to shake things up a bit."

A warmth spread through me that had nothing to do with the wine. "You really think so? Sometimes I worry I'm too different, that I'll never fit in here."

Bennet's eyes locked with mine, his gaze intense. "You fit perfectly," he said softly. "Right here, with me."

My heart pounded as he leaned in, his hand cupping my cheek. When our lips met, it was soft and sweet, tasting of Chardonnay and possibilities. I melted into the kiss, all my doubts and fears fading away in that moment.

When we finally pulled apart, both a little breathless, I couldn't help but grin. "Wow," I murmured.

"Long overdue?" Bennet suggested, his thumb tracing circles on my hand.

I laughed, feeling lighter than I had in months. "Definitely."

As the stars twinkled overhead, we talked and laughed, sharing stories of our pasts and dreams for the future. Bennet told me about his ideas for expanding the winery's event offerings, and I got excited, my mind racing with possibilities.

"Oh!" I exclaimed, an idea striking me. "What if we did a series of seasonal wine and food pairing events? We could showcase local produce and your wines, maybe even partner with some artisans from the craft fair."

Bennet's face lit up. "That's brilliant, Quinn. We could start with a harvest theme, maybe do some interactive elements like grape stomping or blending workshops."

As we bounced ideas back and forth, a thrill pierced my heart. This was why I'd started Quinn Hartley Events, to bring people together, to create magical experiences. And doing it with Bennet, combining our passions and skills, felt like the most natural thing in the world.

The night grew cooler, and Bennet wrapped a soft blanket around our shoulders as we stargazed. I leaned into him, savoring the warmth of his body and the sense of peace that had settled over me.

"Thank you for tonight," I said softly. "It was perfect."

Bennet pressed a kiss to my temple. "Thank you for taking a chance on me. On us."

As we packed up to head back to town, I felt like I was walking on air. We stole glances and shy smiles on the way home. Our hands sat intertwined on the center console.

When we pulled up outside my building, Bennet walked

me to the door. "So," he said, a hint of nervousness in his voice. "What do you say to making this a regular thing? The date nights, I mean. Not necessarily the grape picking, though I'm not opposed to that either."

I laughed, my heart swelling with affection. "I'd love that," I said, standing on my tiptoes to give him a quick kiss. "Goodnight, Bennet."

"Goodnight, Quinn," he murmured, his eyes soft in the dim porch light.

I floated up the stairs to my apartment, feeling like I was in a dream. As I got ready for bed, replaying every moment of the evening in my mind, my phone buzzed with a text from Bennet.

*Already missing you. Sweet dreams, Quinn.*

I hugged the phone to my chest, a giddy smile on my face. For the first time since moving to Doveport, I felt like I truly belonged. Like I'd found my place.

The next morning, I woke up feeling refreshed and energized. I hummed as I made my coffee, ideas for upcoming events swirling in my mind. The collaboration with Bennet and the winery felt like the perfect opportunity to showcase what Quinn Hartley Events could do.

I was just settling down at my desk to sketch out some plans when my phone rang. My heart skipped a beat when I saw the name on the screen: Vivian Astor, my former mentor and one of the top event planners in New York City.

"Vivian?" I answered, surprised. "It's been a while."

"Quinn, darling!" Vivian's crisp, no-nonsense voice came through the line. "I hope I'm not catching you at a bad time. I have some news that I think you'll be very interested in."

I sat up straighter, my pulse quickening. "What kind of news?"

"Well, as you know, I've been looking for someone to take over some of my high-profile clients as I start to scale back my workload. And I've been keeping an eye on your work, Quinn. I have to say, I'm impressed with what you've been doing in that little town of yours."

My mind raced. Was she saying what I thought she was saying?

"I'll cut to the chase," Vivian continued. "I'd like to offer you a position as my associate planner. You'd be working with some of the biggest names in the industry, planning events that would put you on the map. It's the kind of opportunity that could launch your career to the next level."

I felt like she knocked the wind out of me. This was the offer I'd dreamed about when I first started in the industry. Working with Vivian again, in New York City, planning events on a scale I could only imagine in Doveport.

"I... wow, Vivian. I don't know what to say," I stammered.

"Say yes, of course!" Vivian laughed. "Look, I know it's a big decision. You'd have to relocate back to the city, and I'm sure you've started to put down roots in... what was it called? Doveport? But Quinn, this is the chance of a lifetime. Don't let it slip away."

My mind was spinning. Just last night, I felt so sure about my place in Doveport, about my growing relationship with Bennet and the potential of our collaboration. But now...

"Can I have some time to think about it?" I asked, my voice small.

Vivian sighed. "I suppose, but don't take too long. I need an answer by the end of the week. This is your future we're talking about, Quinn. Don't let sentiment cloud your judgment."

After we hung up, I sat at my desk, staring blankly at the plans I'd been so excited about just moments ago. The opportunity Vivian was offering was everything I'd worked for. It was the fast track to becoming a big name in the industry, to proving to everyone (including myself) that I had what it took to make it in the cutthroat world of high-end event planning.

But accepting would mean leaving Doveport. Leaving the life I'd built here. Leaving Bennet.

I picked up my phone, my finger hovering over Bennet's number. I should tell him about the offer, get his perspective. But something held me back. The memory of last night, of how perfect everything had felt, made my chest ache. How could I tell him I was considering leaving, just when we were exploring what we could be together?

Instead, I texted him a quick message: "Had a great time last night. Swamped with work today, talk soon?"

His reply came almost immediately: "Miss you already. Can't wait to see you again. Dinner tomorrow?"

I stared at his message, tears pricking at the corners of my eyes. How had everything gotten so complicated so quickly?

The rest of the day passed in a blur. I tried to focus on work, on the upcoming events I had planned, but my mind kept drifting back to Vivian's offer. I made pro and con lists, researched apartment prices in New York, even looked up the cost of breaking my lease in Doveport. But no matter how many logical arguments I made, I couldn't shake the feeling that I was on the verge of making a huge mistake.

As evening fell, I walked through the streets of Doveport, trying to clear my head. The town was quieting down for the night, the warm glow of streetlights casting a cozy atmosphere. I passed by the bookstore where I lived, the café where Bennet and I had first really talked, the park where he'd shared his ideas for the harvest dinner.

Every corner of this town held a memory, a piece of the life I'd been building. Could I really walk away from all of it?

I ended up at the small dock overlooking the river that ran through town. The water reflected the stars above, a mirror image of the sky. I sat down, dangling my feet over the edge, and tried to sort through the jumble of emotions in my chest.

On one hand, Vivian's offer represented everything I'd thought I wanted when I started my career. The prestige, the challenge, the chance to make a name for myself in the industry. It was the logical next step, the smart career move.

But there was Doveport. There was the warmth of this community that had slowly but surely embraced me. There were the relationships I'd built, the potential I saw for growing my business in a way that felt authentic and meaningful. And there was Bennet, with his kind eyes and his passion for his family's legacy, who made me feel like I could be myself in a way I never had before.

I pulled out my phone, scrolling through the photos from last night. Bennet and I in the vineyard, laughing as we harvested grapes. The candlelit table he'd set up, so romantic and thoughtful. A selfie we'd taken as we stargazed, our faces close together, eyes shining with happiness.

A lump formed in my throat. How could I leave this behind? But then again, how could I turn down the opportunity of a lifetime?

As if on cue, my phone buzzed with a text from Bennet: *Just wanted to say goodnight. Sweet dreams, Quinn. Can't wait to see you tomorrow.*

I clutched the phone to my chest, tears finally spilling over. I had less than a week to make a decision that would change the course of my entire life. Stay in Doveport, pursue this budding relationship with Bennet, and see where my small-town event planning business could go? Or return to New York, work with one of the biggest names in the industry, and potentially skyrocket my career?

The stars twinkled above, offering no answers. The gentle lapping of the river against the dock seemed to echo the turmoil in my heart. As I sat there, torn between two futures, I couldn't help but wonder: was I really ready to choose between my heart and my ambition? And if I did, would I be able to live with the consequences of that choice?

The cool night air sent a shiver down my spine. Or maybe it was the weight of the decision looming over me. I stood up, taking one last look at the peaceful town around me.

# CHAPTER FOUR

*B*ennet
          I wiped the sweat from my brow, squinting against the late afternoon sun as I surveyed the bustling activity in the vineyard. The air was thick with the sweet scent of ripe grapes and the excited chatter of our harvest crew. It should have been a moment of triumph with our first harvest since implementing the new techniques I'd been pushing for. Instead, my stomach churned with a mixture of anxiety and guilt.

"Bennet!" Quinn's voice cut through the noise, and I turned to see her jogging towards me, her auburn hair catching the sunlight. Despite everything, my heart skipped a beat at the sight of her. "I just finished setting up for the tasting event tonight. Is everything okay out here?"

I forced a smile, trying to push down the worry gnawing at me. "Yeah, we're right on schedule. The new sorting system is working like a charm."

Quinn's brow furrowed as she studied my face. "Are you sure? You look stressed."

I hesitated, torn between wanting to confide in her and

not wanting to burden her with my problems. Before I could decide, my phone buzzed in my pocket. I glanced at the screen and felt my stomach drop.

"I'm sorry, I need to take this," I said, already backing away. "It's the doctor's office."

Quinn's eyes widened with concern. But I was already turning away, heading for a quieter spot between the rows of vines.

"Hello?" I answered, my voice tight.

"Mr. Winslow? This is Dr. Patel's office. I'm calling about your grandfather's test results."

My free hand clenched into a fist as I listened to the nurse's calm, professional voice deliver the news I'd been dreading. Grandpa's condition was worse than we'd initially thought. He'd need surgery, followed by an extended recovery period.

As I hung up, I leaned against a nearby trellis, my mind racing. With Grandpa out of commission, the bulk of the winery's management would fall to me. And it couldn't have come at a worse time. We were in the middle of harvest season, with a series of events planned to launch our new wine line.

I took a deep breath, trying to center myself. I could do this. I had to do this. The winery was my family's legacy, and I couldn't let it falter now.

When I made my way back to where I'd left Quinn, I found her deep in conversation with our head vintner, Maria. They both looked up as I approached, concern etched on their faces.

"Bennet?" Quinn said softly. "What's going on?"

I ran a hand through my hair, suddenly feeling the weight of everything pressing down on me. "It's Grandpa," I said, my voice rougher than I intended. "His condition is more serious than we thought. He's going to need surgery."

Quinn's hand flew to her mouth. "Oh, Bennet, I'm so sorry. Is there anything I can do?"

I shook my head, already mentally reorganizing our schedule. "Thanks, but I've got it handled. Maria, can you oversee the rest of today's harvest? I need to head up to the main house and start making some calls."

Maria nodded, her experienced eyes studying me. "Of course, Bennet. Don't worry about a thing down here."

As Maria headed off to direct the crew, Quinn stepped closer, her hand resting lightly on my arm. "Are you sure you don't need any help? I can cancel the tasting event tonight if you need me to."

I briefly thought about accepting her offer. The thought of dealing with a crowd of wine enthusiasts while my mind was reeling with worry about Grandpa and the winery's future was almost unbearable. But I knew how much work Quinn had put into planning this event, how important it was for launching our new collaborative venture.

"No," I said, forcing a smile. "The show must go on, right? This event is too important to cancel. I'll handle things with Grandpa and be there in time for the tasting."

Quinn looked unconvinced, but she nodded. "Okay, if you're sure. But please, Bennet, don't hesitate to let me know if there's anything I can do."

I leaned in and gave her a quick kiss, grateful for her support. "Thanks, Quinn. I'll see you later."

As I walked up to the main house, my mind was already spinning with all the tasks ahead of me. I'd need to contact our distributors, reschedule meetings, and figure out how to cover Grandpa's responsibilities during harvest season.

The next few hours passed in a blur of phone calls and emails. By the time I glanced at my watch and realized I needed to get ready for the tasting event, my head was pounding and my eyes felt gritty from staring at spreadsheets.

I quickly showered and changed into a crisp button-down and slacks, trying to muster up some enthusiasm for the evening ahead. This event was the culmination of months of planning with Quinn, a chance to showcase our new wine line and her event planning skills. I couldn't let my personal worries overshadow that.

When I arrived at the event space of a beautifully renovated barn on the edge of the vineyard, the transformation immediately struck me. Quinn had outdone herself. Twinkling lights hung from the rafters, casting a warm glow over the rustic wood interior. They set up long tables with elegant place settings, each featuring a different wine glass for the tasting flight. The air filled with the soft strains of acoustic guitar and the excited murmur of arriving guests.

I spotted Quinn near the entrance, greeting people with her trademark warm smile. She looked stunning in a deep burgundy dress that complemented the rich colors of the fall decorations. As our eyes met across the room, her smile widened, and I felt a flutter in my chest despite everything else weighing on me.

"There you are," she said as I made my way over to her. "I was starting to worry you wouldn't make it."

I leaned in to kiss her cheek, breathing in the familiar scent of her perfume. "Wouldn't miss it for the world," I said, hoping my voice sounded more confident than I felt. "This place looks amazing, Quinn. You've really outdone yourself."

She beamed at the compliment, but I could see the concern lingering in her eyes. "Thanks. Are you sure you're up for this? I can handle the presentation if you need me to."

I shook my head, squaring my shoulders. "No, I've got it. This is our moment, Quinn. Let's make the most of it."

As the event got underway, I slipped into the familiar role of charming host and passionate winemaker. I led the guests through the tasting, explaining the unique qualities of each wine and the story behind its creation. Quinn seamlessly complemented my presentation, adding details about food pairings and sharing anecdotes about the planning process.

Despite my earlier worries, I genuinely enjoyed the evening. The guests were enthusiastic. The wine was flowing, and Quinn's presence beside me was a constant source of comfort and strength.

It wasn't until later, as we were saying goodbye to the last of the guests, that I overheard a snippet of conversation that made my blood run cold.

"Did you hear?" one woman whispered to her companion. "Apparently, that event planner they brought in from the city is just using the winery to boost her own profile. I heard she's planning to leave for a big job in New York any day now."

I froze, my mind reeling. Quinn, leaving for New York? She had mentioned a job offer. But then again, with everything going on with Grandpa and the winery, when was the last time we'd really talked about her career plans?

I glanced over at Quinn, who was chatting animatedly with a small group of guests. She looked so at home here, so passionate about the work we were doing together. Could she really be planning to leave it all behind?

As the last guests trickled out, Quinn made her way over to me, her face flushed with excitement. "Bennet, can you believe how well that went? I've already had three inquiries about hosting private events here!"

I tried to smile, but my mind was still spinning from

what I'd overheard. "That's great, Quinn. Listen, can we talk for a minute?"

Her expression sobered immediately. "Of course. Is everything okay? Is it about your grandfather?"

I shook my head, leading her to a quiet corner of the room. "No, it's... I overheard something tonight. About you."

Quinn's brow furrowed in confusion. "About me? What do you mean?"

I took a deep breath, hating the doubt that had crept into my voice. "There's a rumor going around that you're planning to leave for a job in New York. Is that true?"

Quinn's eyes widened, and for a moment, she looked like a deer caught in headlights. My heart sank. "Bennet, I..."

Before she could continue, Maria, who burst into the room looking frantic, interrupted us. "Bennet! There you are. We've got a problem with the new sorting equipment. It's jammed, and we can't afford to lose any more time with the harvest."

I closed my eyes for a moment, feeling pulled in a thousand different directions. When I opened them, Quinn was watching me with a mixture of concern and guilt?

"Go," she said softly. "We can talk later."

I hesitated, torn between the urgent needs of the winery and the conversation we desperately needed to have. "Quinn, I..."

She shook her head, giving me a small smile that didn't quite reach her eyes. "It's okay. I understand. The winery comes first."

As I followed Maria out to deal with the latest crisis, I couldn't shake the feeling that I was letting something important slip away. But with Grandpa's health declining, the pressure of the harvest, and now this equipment malfunction, I didn't know how to balance it all.

The next few hours were a blur of troubleshooting and manual sorting. By the time we got the equipment back up and running, the sky was lightening with the first hints of dawn. I stumbled back to my cabin, exhausted and covered in grape juice, my mind still churning with worries about the winery, Grandpa, and now, Quinn.

As I collapsed onto my bed, still fully clothed, I wondered how long I could keep this up? Something had to give, but I was terrified of what that might mean. The winery was my family's legacy, my responsibility. But Quinn had become a part of me in a way I hadn't expected, hadn't even known I was missing until she came into my life.

I closed my eyes, and the weight of decisions yet to be made pressed down on me. As sleep finally claimed me, one thought echoed through my mind: I couldn't lose either of them. But how could I possibly keep both?

The shrill ring of my phone jolted me awake for what felt like minutes later. I fumbled for it, squinting at the too-bright screen. It was barely past noon.

"Hello?" I croaked, my voice rough with sleep.

"Bennet?" It was Quinn, her voice tight with an emotion I couldn't quite place. "I think we need to talk. Can you meet me at the overlook in an hour?"

My stomach clenched. The overlook was where we'd had our first real conversation, where I'd first realized there might be something special between us. "Yeah, of course. Quinn, about last night..."

"We'll talk when we meet," she said, cutting me off gently. "Just please be there, okay?"

As I hung up, I felt a sense of dread settling over me. I dragged myself out of bed, wincing at my reflection in the mirror. Dark circles under my eyes, hair a mess, still wearing my grape-stained clothes from yesterday. I looked about as good as I felt.

After a quick shower and change of clothes, I headed out to the vineyard. The day was beautiful, crisp and clear, with just a hint of that distinctive fall chill in the air. Any other time, I would have appreciated it, to breathe in the scent of ripening grapes and feel the warmth of the sun on my face. Today, I barely noticed as I made my way to the overlook.

Quinn was already there when I arrived, perched on the old wooden fence that marked the edge of our property. She was gazing out over the rolling hills of the vineyard, the wind gently tousling her hair. For a moment, I just stood there, drinking in the sight of her. How had I gotten so lucky? And how had I messed it up so quickly?

"Hey," I said softly, not wanting to startle her.

She turned, and the look in her eyes made my heart ache. There was sadness there, and uncertainty, but also a determination that I recognized all too well.

"Bennet," she said, attempting a smile that didn't quite reach her eyes. "Thanks for coming."

I moved to stand beside her, close but not touching. "Quinn, about last night... I'm sorry I didn't get a chance to talk to you properly. Things got crazy with the equipment malfunction, and..."

She held up a hand, stopping me. "It's okay. I understand. The winery has to come first right now."

The way she said it, like it was a foregone conclusion, made something twist in my chest. "Quinn, that's not... I mean, yes, the winery is important, but you're important too."

She sighed, turning to face me fully. "Am I, Bennet? Because lately, it feels like I'm always coming in second. To the winery, to your family obligations, to everything."

I opened my mouth to protest, but she continued before I could speak.

"And I get it, I do. This place is your family's legacy. It's a huge responsibility. But Bennet, where do I fit into all of that?"

I reached for her hand, relieved when she didn't pull away. "Quinn, you fit everywhere. These past few months, working with you, being with you. Has been amazing. I don't want to lose that."

She squeezed my hand, but her eyes were sad. "I don't want to lose it either. But Bennet, I can't keep putting my life on hold. My career, my dreams..."

And there it was. The job offer I'd overheard about. "Is this about New York?" I asked, hating how small my voice sounded. "Are you really thinking of leaving?"

Quinn's eyes widened in surprise. "How did you...? Never mind. Yes, I got an offer. From my old mentor in New York. It's a big opportunity, Bennet."

I felt like the ground was shifting beneath my feet. "When were you going to tell me?"

She looked away, guilt flashing across her face. "I was going to tell you last night, after the event. But then everything happened with your grandfather, and the equipment malfunction... it never seemed like the right time."

I let go of her hand, running my fingers through my hair in frustration. "So what, you were just going to leave? Without even giving us a chance to figure this out?"

"No!" Quinn exclaimed, her eyes flashing. "That's not... Bennet, I'm telling you now. I'm trying to figure this out. But I need to know where I stand with you, with all of this." She gestured to the vineyard spread out below us.

I took a deep breath, trying to calm the storm of emotions raging inside me. "Quinn, I love you," I said, the words tumbling out before I could stop them. It was the first time I'd said it out loud, but I realized as soon as I did it was true. "I love you, and I want you to be a part of my life, of all of this."

Her eyes softened, and for a moment, I thought everything might be okay. But then she spoke, her voice barely above a whisper. "I love you too, Bennet. But is that enough? Can you really give me a place here, when you're already stretched so thin?"

I wanted to say yes, to promise her the world. But I didn't know. With Grandpa's health declining, the pressure of the harvest, and all the new initiatives we'd started. I was barely keeping my head above water as it was.

"I want to," I said finally, my voice rough with emotion. "I want to make this work, Quinn. I just need some time to figure out how."

She nodded, a single tear slipping down her cheek. "I understand. But Bennet, I can't wait forever. I have to give Vivian an answer by the end of the week."

The end of the week. Just a few days to figure out how to balance everything I cared about the winery, my family, and now, Quinn. It felt impossible.

"Okay," I said, pulling her into my arms. She came willingly, burying her face in my chest.

As we stood there, holding each other with the vineyard spread out before us, I couldn't shake the feeling that we were standing on the edge of a precipice. One wrong move, and everything could come crashing down.

My phone buzzed in my pocket. Probably Maria, with another crisis to handle. Quinn stiffened in my arms, and I knew she'd felt it too.

"You should get that," she said, pulling away slightly.

I shook my head, tightening my hold on her. "No. Not right now. Right now, this is what matters."

She looked up at me, a glimmer of hope in her eyes. "Yeah?"

I nodded, leaning down to kiss her softly. "Yeah. We're going to figure this out, Quinn. I promise."

We walked back towards the winery, hand in hand, with aa renewed sense of determination. I didn't know how yet, but I was going to make this work. The winery, my family, Quinn, were all part of my world now, and I would let none of them slip away without a fight.

## CHAPTER FIVE

$Q$uinn

I twirled, letting the crisp autumn breeze catch my skirt and send leaves swirling around my feet. The Autumn Leaves Festival was in full swing, and I couldn't remember the last time I'd felt this carefree. Bennet's warm laugh reached my ears, and I turned to see him watching me with a mix of amusement and adoration.

"Having fun?" he asked, reaching out to pluck a leaf from my hair.

I grinned, catching his hand and pulling him closer. "More than I've had in ages. Thanks for convincing me to come today."

He pressed a quick kiss to my forehead. "My pleasure. Though I have to admit, I had an ulterior motive."

I raised an eyebrow. "Oh?"

Bennet's eyes sparkled with excitement. "I thought it might give us some inspiration for our next big event at the winery. Just look at all this!" He gestured around us at the bustling festival grounds.

I had to admit, the organizers had outdone themselves.

Strings of twinkling lights crisscrossed overhead, creating a warm glow as the afternoon light faded. Vendors lined the streets, offering everything from hot apple cider to hand-crafted pottery. The scent of cinnamon and wood smoke filled the air, and a jaunty folk tune played somewhere nearby, while vendors lined the streets offering everything from hot apple cider to handcrafted pottery.

"It is pretty magical," I agreed, my event planner brain already whirring with possibilities. "Oh! What if we did a twilight harvest event? We could set up lights through the vineyard, and have different stations for wine tasting paired with seasonal treats."

Bennet's face lit up. "That's brilliant, Quinn! We could even incorporate some of the local artisans, maybe have them do demonstrations or workshops."

We spent the next hour wandering through the festival, pointing out details we liked and brainstorming ways to incorporate them into our own events. It felt so natural, the way our ideas flowed together, each of us building on the other's thoughts. This was what I loved about working with Bennet and the easy synergy, the shared passion.

As we approached a booth selling hand-poured candles, I spotted a familiar face in the crowd. My stomach dropped. "Oh no," I muttered.

Bennet followed my gaze. "What is it?"

Before I could answer, the woman I'd spotted made her way over to us, a predatory smile on her face. "Quinn Hartley, as I live and breathe! What are you doing all the way out here in the sticks?"

I plastered on my best professional smile. "Vivian! What a surprise. I didn't expect to see you here."

Vivian Astor, my former mentor and one of the top event planners in New York City, air-kissed my cheeks before turning her razor-sharp gaze on Bennet. "And who's this handsome gentleman?"

Tension radiated off Bennet as I made the introductions. "Vivian, this is Bennet Winslow, my partner. Bennet, this is Vivian Astor, my former mentor in New York."

Vivian's eyebrows shot up at the word 'partner,' and I could see the wheels turning in her head. "Partner? How quaint. Tell me, Bennet, what is it you do?"

"I own Winslow Vineyards," Bennet replied, his voice cool but polite. "Quinn and I have been collaborating on a series of events there."

"A vineyard?" Vivian's tone dripped with condescension. "How lovely. Quinn always did have a soft spot for rustic charm."

My cheeks burned with a mixture of embarrassment and anger rising in my chest. "Actually, Vivian, our last event was a huge success. We've had inquiries from all over the region about hosting similar experiences."

Vivian's smile didn't quite reach her eyes. "Is that so? Well, isn't that exciting for you both. You know, Quinn, I was just thinking about you the other day. The Harrington account, you remember them, don't you? They're looking to do a series of wine-themed events in the city. I immediately thought of you."

My heart skipped a beat. The Harringtons were a big deal with old money, major influencers in the New York social scene. Landing their account would be a massive boost for any event planner.

"That's... wow, Vivian. That's incredibly generous of you to think of me," I stammered, surprised.

Vivian waved her hand dismissively. "Oh, it's nothing. I just hate to see all that talent of yours going to waste out here in the middle of nowhere. Why don't you come back to the city for a few weeks? We could collaborate on the pitch, just like old times."

Bennet stiffened beside me. "Quinn's talent isn't going to waste," he said, his voice tight. "We have big plans for the winery's event program."

Vivian's gaze flicked to Bennet, then back to me, a knowing smirk playing at her lips. "I'm sure you do, dear. But Quinn, darling, let's be realistic. There's only so far you can go with local events. You were made for bigger things."

I opened my mouth to respond, but no words came out. Part of me wanted to defend our work, to tell Vivian about all the exciting ideas we had. But another part, a part I wasn't proud of, preened at her praise, at the idea that I was *made for bigger things*.

Bennet's hand found mine, squeezing gently. The warmth of his touch grounded me, reminding me of everything we'd built together.

"Thank you for thinking of me, Vivian," I said finally, finding my voice. "But I'm happy with the work I'm doing here. Bennet and I have some really exciting projects in the works."

Vivian's smile turned brittle. "Well, if you change your mind, you know how to reach me. The offer stands for now." She air-kissed my cheeks again before melting back into the crowd, leaving a cloud of expensive perfume and doubt in her wake.

For a moment, Bennet and I stood in silence, the festive atmosphere around us feeling suddenly hollow.

"So," Bennet said finally, his voice carefully neutral. "That was your former mentor."

I nodded, unable to meet his eyes. "Yeah. Sorry about that. Vivian can be intense."

"She certainly seemed eager to get you back to New

York," Bennet observed, and I could hear the question he wasn't asking.

I sighed, finally looking up at him. "Bennet, I'm not going anywhere. You know that, right? What we're doing at the winery, it's important to me."

He searched my face, and I could see the doubt lingering in his eyes. "Is it enough, though? Quinn, if you're holding yourself back because of me, because of us..."

"No," I said firmly, gripping his hands in mine. "That's not it at all. I love what we're creating together. It's just..." I trailed off, struggling to put my feelings into words.

Bennet's expression softened. "It's okay to be flattered by her offer, Quinn. I get it. The Harringtons are a big deal."

I nodded, grateful for his understanding. "They are. But that doesn't mean I want to drop everything and run back to New York. It's just... sometimes I wonder if I'm making the right choices, you know? If I'm living up to my potential."

Bennet pulled me into a hug, and I melted into his embrace, breathing in the familiar scent of him with a mix of cedar and grapevines that had become home to me.

"You're the most talented, creative person I know," he murmured into my hair. "And I know you're going to do amazing things, whether that's here or anywhere else."

I pulled back slightly, meeting his gaze. "I want it to be here," I said softly. "With you. I guess I needed the reminder of why I left New York in the first place. The constant competition, the pressure to always be chasing the next big thing. It's exhausting."

Bennet nodded, a small smile tugging at his lips. "Well, I can't promise we won't have our share of pressure at the winery, especially with harvest season coming up. But I can promise that at the end of the day, there will always be a good glass of wine and a sunset view waiting for you."

I laughed, feeling some of the tension ease from my shoulders. "Now that sounds like my kind of career path."

As we resumed our stroll through the festival, hand in hand, I tried to shake off the lingering unease from Vivian's appearance. But her words kept echoing in my mind: *There's only so far you can go with local events.*

Was she right? Were Bennet and I limiting ourselves by focusing on the winery and the local community? Or was there a way to think bigger while still staying true to what we loved about our work?

We stopped at a booth selling artisanal cheeses, and as Bennet chatted with the vendor about potential pairings for our wines, an idea formed in my mind.

"Bennet," I said, tugging on his sleeve excitedly. "What if we didn't limit ourselves to just the winery for our events?"

He turned to me, curiosity in his eyes. "What do you mean?"

"Well, look at this festival," I gestured around us. "It's not just about the leaves, right? It's a celebration of everything this region has to offer with the food, the crafts, the music. What if we did something similar, but centered on wine culture?"

Bennet's eyes lit up as he caught on to my train of thought. "Like a traveling wine festival?"

I nodded enthusiastically. "Exactly! We could partner with other vineyards in the region, bring in local artisans and chefs. We could even do pop-up events in bigger cities to showcase what our area has to offer."

"Quinn, that's brilliant," Bennet said, pulling me in for a quick kiss. "It would be a way to grow our reach without losing touch with what makes our events special."

As the sun set and the festival lights twinkled to life around us, a small voice in the back of my mind whispered a warning. Were we getting ahead of ourselves? Could we really pull off something this ambitious?

I pushed the doubts aside, focusing instead on Bennet's enthusiasm as he talked about potential locations and themes. We could do this. We had to do this. Because if we didn't at least try, I knew I'd always wonder what might have been.

As we made our way back to the car, arms laden with purchases from various vendors, Bennet suddenly stopped short. "Quinn," he said, his voice tight. "Look."

I followed his gaze and felt my stomach drop. There, plastered on a community bulletin board, was a flyer advertising an upcoming wine tasting event in the city. An event hosted by none other than Vivian Astor, featuring wines from some of our biggest local competitors.

"How did she..." I trailed off, my mind racing. Some of those vineyards had been in talks with us about our festival idea. Had Vivian somehow gotten wind of our plans?

Bennet set his jaw in a hard line. "She works fast, I'll give her that."

A wave of guilt washed over me. "Bennet, I swear I didn't say anything to her about our ideas. I would never-"

He turned to me, his expression softening. "I know, Quinn. I trust you. But this changes things."

I nodded, my earlier excitement now tempered by a heavy dose of reality. "We'll have to move quickly if we want to get ahead of this. Are you sure you're ready for that? With everything else going on at the winery..."

Bennet was quiet for a moment, his gaze distant. When he finally spoke, his voice was determined. "We can't let this opportunity slip away. If we don't do it now, someone else will. Whether it's Vivian or another competitor."

I squeezed his hand, feeling a mix of excitement and trepidation. "Okay. Then let's do it. First thing tomorrow, we'll start reaching out to potential partners, drawing up a business plan."

As we drove home, the twinkling lights of the festival fading in the rearview mirror, I couldn't shake the feeling that we were standing on the edge of something big. Something that could either make or break everything we'd been working towards.

I glanced over at Bennet, his profile illuminated by the dashboard lights. He looked deep in thought, his brow furrowed slightly. I knew he was probably running through mental calculations, trying to figure out how to balance this new venture with the demands of the winery.

"Hey," I said softly, reaching over to rest my hand on his knee. "We've got this, right?"

He turned to me, a small smile breaking through his serious expression. "Yeah," he said, covering my hand with his own. "We've got this."

As we pulled up to my apartment, Bennet put the car in park but made no move to get out. "Quinn," he said, his voice serious. "Before we dive into all of this tomorrow, I need to know. Are you sure this is what you want? Because if any part of you is still thinking about New York, about Vivian's offer..."

I took a deep breath, really considering his question. Was this what I wanted? To tie my future so close to Bennet, to the winery, to this small town that had become my home?

"Yes," I said finally, surprised by the certainty in my voice. "This is exactly what I want. You, me, building something amazing together. It won't be easy, and I'm sure there will be moments when I doubt myself. But at the end of the day, this feels right in a way that chasing the next big thing in New York never did."

Bennet's smile was like the sun breaking through clouds. He leaned over, cupping my face in his hands, and kissed me with a passion that left me breathless.

When we finally parted, he rested his forehead against mine. "I love you, Quinn Hartley. And I can't wait to see what we create together."

I climbed the stairs to my apartment, already mentally drafting emails and to-do lists. As I reached for my keys, my phone buzzed in my pocket. A text from an unknown number.

My blood ran cold as I read the message:

*Quinn, darling. I hope you know what you're getting into. The wine industry can be cutthroat, and not everyone plays fair. If you change your mind about my offer, you know where to find me. - V*

I stared at the screen, my earlier confidence wavering. What did Vivian know we didn't? And how far was she willing to go to get what she wanted?

# CHAPTER SIX

*B*ennet

I wiped the sweat from my brow, my hands trembling slightly as I adjusted the last string of twinkling lights. The new event space, hidden away in a secluded corner of the vineyard, was finally ready. I stepped back, taking in the rustic-chic barn we'd transformed over the past few weeks. The polished wood gleamed in the early morning light, and the scent of fresh paint mingled with the crisp autumn air.

"It's perfect," I murmured to myself, a mix of pride and nervousness swirling in my chest. This space was more than just an addition to the winery. It was a declaration of my commitment to Quinn and our shared dreams.

My phone buzzed in my pocket, jolting me back to reality. It was Maria, our head vintner.

"Bennet, where are you? The first guests for the Thanksgiving feast will be arriving in an hour, and we still need to go over the wine pairings!"

I cursed under my breath. In my excitement over Quinn's surprise, I'd almost forgotten about the community feast we were hosting today. "I'll be right there," I promised, taking one last look at the event space before jogging back towards the main buildings.

The winery was a hive of activity when I arrived. Staff bustled about, setting up tables and arranging centerpieces. The kitchen was a whirlwind of savory aromas, with our chef, Antonio, barking orders as he orchestrated the massive meal.

I found Maria in the tasting room, surrounded by bottles and notepads. Her eyebrows shot up as I entered. "Cutting it a little close, aren't we?"

I grinned sheepishly. "Sorry, I got caught up with a project. But I'm all yours now. Let's nail these pairings."

We dove into work, discussing which wines would best complement each course of the feast. As we debated the merits of our Pinot Noir versus our Syrah for the turkey course, I marveled at how far we'd come.

Just a few months ago, I'd been drowning in the responsibilities of running the winery, torn between tradition and innovation. But since fully embracing my role and bringing Quinn into our world, everything had changed. Her fresh perspective and boundless creativity had breathed new life into the business, and into me.

"Earth to Bennet," Maria's voice cut through my reverie. "You still with me?"

I blinked, focusing back on the task at hand. "Yeah, sorry. Let's go with the Pinot. It's got the acidity to cut through the richness of the turkey and gravy."

Maria nodded approvingly. "Good call. Now, about the dessert course..."

We finished just as the first guests arrived. I smoothed down my shirt and put on my best host smile, greeting familiar faces from the community. Local farmers, shopkeepers, and families streamed in, all bringing a dish to share alongside our wine and turkey.

As I directed people to the beautifully decorated barn where we'd be hosting the feast, I scanned the crowd for Quinn. My heart skipped a beat when I finally spotted her, her auburn hair catching the sunlight as she chatted animatedly with Mrs. Henderson from the local bakery.

I made my way over, unable to keep the grin off my face. "Ladies," I said, nodding to Mrs. Henderson before turning to Quinn. "You look beautiful."

Quinn's eyes sparkled as she smiled up at me. "Thanks. This is amazing, Bennet. I can't believe how many people showed up."

I shrugged, trying to play it cool despite the warmth spreading through my chest at her praise. "Well, we do have the best wine in the county. That's a pretty big draw."

She laughed, swatting my arm playfully. "And the most modest winemaker, clearly."

As more guests arrived, Quinn and I fell into our usual rhythm, working the room together. She had a knack for putting people at ease, drawing out even the shyest attendees with her genuine interest and quick wit. I constantly glanced her way, marveling at how seamlessly she'd integrated herself into this world that had once been solely mine.

The feast itself was a roaring success. The food was delicious, and the wine flowed freely, and the barn echoed with laughter and conversation. As I looked out over the sea of happy faces, I felt a surge of pride. This was what I'd always dreamed the winery could be, a place that brought people together, that celebrated not just our wines but our community.

As the meal wound down, I clinked my glass, calling for attention. "I'd like to propose a toast," I said, my voice carrying over the crowd. "To family, both old and new. To traditions honored and innovations embraced. And to all of you, for being part of this journey with us."

A chorus of "Hear, hear!" rang out as glasses clinked. I caught Quinn's eye across the room, and the look of love and pride on her face nearly took my breath away.

As the guests dispersed, helping to clean up in that small-town way that still warmed my heart, I made my way to Quinn's side. "Hey," I said softly, taking her hand. "Can I borrow you for a minute? There's something I want to show you."

She looked at me curiously, but nodded. "Of course. Lead the way."

My heart pounded as I guided her out of the barn and down a winding path through the vineyard. The sun was setting, painting the sky in brilliant shades of orange and pink. As we walked, I babbled nervously about the harvest, the wines we were aging, anything to distract from the butterflies in my stomach.

Quinn squeezed my hand, looking up at me with a mix of amusement and concern. "Bennet, what's going on? You're acting strange."

I took a deep breath, steeling myself. "I've been working on something. A surprise for you. For us, really."

We rounded a bend in the path, and suddenly, there it was. The new event space lit up against the darkening sky like a beacon. I heard Quinn's sharp intake of breath and held my own, waiting for her reaction.

"Bennet," she whispered, her eyes wide as she took in the rustic-chic structure. "What is this?"

I guided her closer, my words tumbling out in a rush of excitement. "It's an event space. For us. For Quinn Hartley Events and Winslow Vineyards. I know we talked about expanding, about doing more destination events, and I thought... well, I thought this could be a start."

Quinn strolled around the building, her hand trailing along the weathered wood. "You built this? For me?"

I nodded, suddenly feeling unsure. "For us. I mean, if you want. I know it's a big step, and if it's too much, too soon..."

She turned to me then, and I was stunned to see tears in her eyes. "Bennet Oak Winslow," she said, her voice thick with emotion. "This is the most incredible thing anyone has ever done for me."

Relief and joy flooded through me. I closed the distance between us, cupping her face in my hands. "I love you, Quinn. And I love the life we're building together. I want to give you, give us, a place to make all those amazing ideas of yours come to life."

Quinn's smile was radiant as she wrapped her arms around my neck. "I love you too. And I can't wait to see what we create here."

As I leaned in to kiss her, the last light of day fading around us, I felt a sense of rightness settle over me. This was where I belonged, with Quinn, building something beautiful together.

But the buzz of my phone interrupted our moment of bliss. I reluctantly pulled away, fishing the device from my pocket. My stomach dropped as I read the message from Maria:

*SOS. Vivian Astor is here. Says she has a proposition for us. What do you want me to do?*

I looked up at Quinn, seeing the concern in her eyes as she registered the change in my expression. "What is it?" she asked.

I swallowed hard, the joy of our moment suddenly overshadowed by a looming threat. "Vivian's here," I said, watching Quinn's face pale. "And apparently, she has a proposition for us."

Quinn's jaw set in determination. "Then I guess we better go hear what she has to say."

The walk back to the main building felt both endless and far too short. My mind raced with possibilities. What could Vivian want? And why show up unannounced, today of all days?

Quinn's hand tightened on mine as we approached the tasting room. Through the window, I could see Vivian, impeccably dressed as always, perched on a stool at the bar. Maria hovered nearby, looking uncomfortable.

"Ready?" I asked Quinn, pausing at the door.

She took a deep breath, squaring her shoulders. "As I'll ever be."

We entered together, presenting a united front. Vivian's perfectly manicured eyebrows rose as she took us in.

"Well, well," she purred, her gaze flicking between us. "If it isn't the dynamic duo. How quaint."

Quinn stiffened beside me but kept my voice level as I addressed our uninvited guest. "Vivian. This is unexpected. What brings you to our neck of the woods?"

Vivian's smile was sharp as she reached for her handbag. "Business, of course. I have a proposition that I think you'll both find very interesting."

She pulled out a sleek folder and laid it on the bar. "I represent a group of investors who are very interested in expanding their portfolio into the wine industry. Specifically, they're looking to acquire boutique wineries with potential."

My stomach clenched. "Acquire?"

Vivian nodded, her eyes gleaming. "They're prepared to make a very generous offer. Enough for you to expand your operations significantly, modernize your equipment. Maybe even open a tasting room in the city."

Quinn's hand slipped into mine again, a silent show of support. "And what would that mean for us? For our staff?"

Vivian waved a hand dismissively. "Oh, you'd stay on to manage things, of course. With some oversight from the board, naturally. As for the staff, well, I'm sure some restructuring would be necessary, but that's just business."

I glanced at Quinn, seeing my mix of shock and indignation mirrored in her eyes. "I appreciate the offer, Vivian, but I'm not interested in selling the winery. This isn't just a business to me. It's my family's legacy."

Vivian's smile didn't waver, but I saw a flash of something cold in her eyes. "I thought you might say that. Which is why I came prepared with a little incentive."

She pulled another document from her bag, sliding it across the bar towards Quinn. "This is a contract for a series of high-profile events in New York. The kind of exposure that could launch Quinn Hartley Events into the stratosphere. All you have to do, Quinn dear, is convince your partner here to see reason."

It felt like someone had punched me in the gut. Vivian was trying to use Quinn against me, to drive a wedge between us. I turned to Quinn, my heart in my throat, half-expecting to see temptation in her eyes.

But Quinn didn't even glance at the contract. Her gaze fixed on Vivian, her voice steady as she spoke. "I'm not interested, Vivian. My place is here, with Bennet and the winery. We're building something special, something that means more than just profit margins and high-profile clients."

Pride and love swelled in my chest. I squeezed Quinn's hand, unable to keep the smile off my face.

Vivian's expression hardened. "Don't be foolish, Quinn.

This is the opportunity of a lifetime. Are you really going to throw away your career for some country romance?"

Quinn lifted her chin, her voice firm. "I'm not throwing anything away. I'm choosing the life and the work that makes me happy. Now, I think it's time for you to leave."

For a moment, Vivian looked genuinely taken aback. Then her mask of cool professionalism slipped back into place. "Very well. But don't come crying to me when this little experiment of yours falls apart. The offer won't be on the table forever."

She gathered her things and swept out of the tasting room, the click of her heels echoing in the sudden silence.

As the door swung shut behind her, I turned to Quinn, a mix of emotions swirling in my chest. "Quinn. Thank you. For choosing us. But are you sure? What she was offering..."

Quinn silenced me with a kiss, soft and sure. When she pulled back, her eyes were shining. "I've never been more sure of anything in my life. This, right here? It's everything I want."

I pulled her close, burying my face in her hair. "I love you," I murmured. "So much."

She laughed softly, her breath warm against my neck. "I love you too. Now, how about we go back to that beautiful new event space and start planning our first official Quinn Hartley Events at Winslow Vineyards extravaganza?"

I grinned, already feeling the spark of excitement that always came when we put our heads together. "Lead the way, partner."

As we walked back through the vineyard, the stars twinkling overhead, I felt a sense of peace settle over me. Vivian's visit had been a shock, but it had also crystallized something for me. This life Quinn and I were building together wasn't just about the winery or the events. It was about creating something meaningful, something that brought joy not just to us but to our entire community.

We reached the new event space, and I couldn't help but smile as Quinn immediately started pacing, her eyes alight with ideas. "Okay, so for our first event, I'm thinking we go big. A winter wonderland theme. We could do an ice wine tasting, maybe partner with some local artisans for a holiday market."

I leaned against the doorframe, content to watch her in her element. This was what I'd hoped for when I built this place, to see Quinn's creativity and passion unleashed.

"Oh!" she exclaimed, turning to me with that infectious grin I loved so much. "What if we did a New Year's Eve bash? Ring in the new year with a toast using that special sparkling wine you've been working on?"

I pushed off the doorframe, crossing to her and pulling her into my arms. "I think that sounds perfect," I said, pressing a kiss to her forehead. "A celebration of new beginnings."

Quinn's arms wound around my waist as she looked up at me, her expression soft. "You know, when I first came to Doveport, I never imagined this is where I'd end up. But now? I can't imagine being anywhere else."

I thought about how close we'd come to losing this, how easily Vivian's offer could have torn us apart if we weren't so sure of what we had together. "I'm so glad you stayed," I murmured. "That you took a chance on this place. On me."

Quinn's smile was radiant. "Best decision I ever made."

# CHAPTER SEVEN

Quinn

I stood in the doorway of our new event space, my heart swelling with pride as I watched Bennet fuss over the last-minute details. The warm glow of the setting sun filtered through the windows, casting a golden hue over the rustic-chic decor we'd spent weeks perfecting. It was December 5th, 2024, and we were about to host our first official event in this space as a holiday wine tasting that would showcase both Winslow Vineyards' finest offerings and my event planning skills.

"Babe, do you think we need more twinkle lights over here?" Bennet called out, his brow furrowed in concentration as he stood on a ladder, adjusting a string of lights.

I couldn't help but chuckle. "Bennet Oak Winslow, if we add any more lights, we'll be visible from space." I crossed the room, placing a hand on the ladder to steady it. "It's perfect. You're perfect."

He looked down at me, that crooked grin I'd fallen in love with spreading across his face. "Just trying to make sure everything's as sparkly as your eyes when you talk about your event ideas."

A blush warmed my cheeks. Even after all this time, Bennet still could make me feel like a love-struck teenager. "Smooth talker," I teased, offering him my hand as he descended the ladder.

As Bennet's feet hit the ground, he pulled me into his arms, and I melted into his embrace. For a moment, we just stood there, savoring the quiet before the storm of guests arrived. I breathed in his familiar scent of a mix of cedar, grapes, and marveled at how far we'd come.

It seemed like only yesterday that I'd arrived in Doveport, a city girl with big dreams and a chip on her shoulder. I'd been so determined to prove myself, to show the world that Quinn Hartley could make it on her own. But somewhere along the way, between autumn festivals and wine tastings, I'd learned that there was strength in partnership, in letting someone else in.

"Penny for your thoughts?" Bennet murmured, his chin resting on top of my head.

I pulled back slightly, looking up into those warm brown eyes that had become my home. "Just thinking about how much has changed. How much we've changed."

Bennet nodded, a soft smile playing on his lips. "For the better, I hope?"

"Definitely for the better," I assured him, reaching up to brush a wayward curl from his forehead. "You know, when I first met you, I thought you were just some stuffy winemaker stuck in his ways."

He let out a laugh with the sound rumbling through his chest. "And I thought you were a city slicker who'd run screaming back to New York at the first sight of a grape press."

I grinned, remembering our early clashes and misunderstandings. "Look at us now. Partners in every sense of the word."

Bennet's expression grew serious, his hands coming up to cup my face. "I wouldn't have it any other way, Quinn. You've brought so much light into my life, into this winery. Sometimes I still can't believe you chose to stay here with me."

I leaned into his touch, feeling a familiar warmth spread through my chest. "Bennet, staying here with you was the easiest decision I've ever made. And the best one."

As if on cue, the last rays of sunlight burst through the windows, bathing us in a golden glow. It felt like a sign, a cosmic nod of approval of our journey together.

"Come on," I said, taking Bennet's hand and leading him towards the French doors that opened onto a small patio overlooking the vineyard. "Let's watch the sunset before the guests arrive."

We stepped out into the crisp December air, and I shivered slightly. Without a word, Bennet shrugged off his jacket and draped it over my shoulders. It was such a simple gesture, but it spoke volumes about the man he was - always thinking of others, always taking care of those around him.

As we leaned against the railing, watching the sun dip below the horizon, painting the sky in vibrant oranges and pinks, I reflected on the past year. The challenges we'd faced, the victories we'd celebrated, and the love that had grown between us through it all.

"You know," I said, breaking the comfortable silence, "a year ago, if someone had told me I'd be standing here, about to host a sold-out holiday wine tasting at my boyfriend's family vineyard, I would have laughed in their face."

Bennet chuckled, his arm tightening around my waist.

"And if someone had told me I'd be madly in love with a city girl who could pair wines better than some sommeliers I know, I probably would have choked on my Cabernet."

I elbowed him playfully. "Hey, I resent that. I could always pair wines well. I just... might not have known how to prune a vine to save my life."

"Might not have?" Bennet raised an eyebrow. "Darling, I love you, but I still don't trust you with the pruning shears."

We both laughed, the sound carrying across the quiet vineyard. As our laughter faded, I turned to face Bennet, suddenly feeling the weight of all we'd built together.

"Bennet," I said, my voice soft but sure, "I want you to know how grateful I am. For everything. For taking a chance on me, for pushing me to be better, for loving me even when I was being stubborn and difficult."

Bennet's eyes softened, and he pulled me closer. "Quinn, you don't have to thank me for loving you. It's as natural as breathing." He paused, a mischievous glint appearing in his eyes. "Even when you're being stubborn and difficult, which, let's be honest, is at least 60% of the time."

I swatted his chest, but I couldn't keep the grin off my face. "I'm trying to have a moment here, you goof."

He caught my hand, bringing it to his lips for a gentle kiss. "I know, I'm sorry. Please, continue."

I took a deep breath, gathering my thoughts. "What I'm trying to say is, I'm all in, Bennet. With you, with the winery, with this life we're building together. I know I've had my doubts in the past, and there have been times when I've wondered if I was making the right choice. But standing here, now, I've never been more certain of anything in my life."

Bennet was quiet for a moment, and I saw a sheen of

tears in his eyes. When he spoke, his voice was thick with emotion. "Quinn Autumn Hartley, you are the best thing that's ever happened to me. To this winery. You brought fresh ideas and energy when we needed it most. You pushed me out of my comfort zone and showed me that change could be good. But more than that, you've become my partner in every sense of the word. I can't imagine doing any of this without you by my side."

Tears pricked at the corners of my own eyes. "So, I guess we're stuck with each other then?"

Bennet laughed, pulling me in for a kiss that left me breathless. "Looks like it. Think you can handle a lifetime of pruning lessons and wine tastings?"

"Hmm," I pretended to consider, tapping my chin thoughtfully. "Will there be more moments like this? Sunsets and sappy declarations of love?"

"Oh, I think I can arrange that," Bennet murmured, leaning in for another kiss.

The sound of car doors interrupted us slamming in the distance. Our first guests had arrived.

"Ready to wow them with your event planning magic?" Bennet asked, offering me his arm.

I took a deep breath, feeling a familiar thrill of excitement run through me. This was it - the moment we'd been working towards for months. Our first official event in the new space, a perfect blend of Winslow tradition and Quinn Hartley innovation.

"Let's do this," I said, linking my arm through his.

As we made our way back into the event space, a sense of anticipation flooded me for what the future held. We had big plans for the coming year with expanding our event offerings, potentially even taking our wine festival idea on the road. But more than that, I anticipated the little moments of us enjoying quiet evenings in the vineyard, having impromptu dance parties in the wine cellar, and spending lazy Sunday mornings planning our next big adventure.

The first guests trickled in, exclaiming over the beautifully decorated space. I slipped easily into host mode, greeting people with warm smiles and guiding them towards the tasting stations we'd set up around the room. Bennet was in his element, regaling guests with stories about each wine's unique characteristics and the history behind our vineyard.

As the evening wore on, I constantly sought out Bennet in the crowd, our eyes meeting across the room in moments of shared joy and pride. This was what we'd built together - not just an event space or a business, but a community. A family.

Later, as the last guests were saying their goodbyes, Bennet found me by the bar, where I was jotting down notes for future improvements.

"So," he said, sliding an arm around my waist, "I'd say that was a smashing success."

I leaned into him, feeling a wave of contentment wash over me. "It really was, wasn't it? Did you see Mrs. Henderson's face when she tried the ice wine? I thought she was going to propose marriage on the spot."

Bennet laughed, the sound rich and warm. "Well, she'll have to get in line. I've got dibs on you."

I turned in his arms, looping my hands around his neck. "Is that so, Mr. Winslow? Are you planning on making an honest woman out of me?"

The moment the words left my mouth, I felt a flutter of panic. We hadn't really talked about marriage, not seriously. But instead of looking spooked, Bennet's eyes sparkled with mischief and something deeper, something that made my heart race.

"Maybe I am," he said softly, his thumb tracing circles on my lower back. "Would that be something you'd be interested in? Someday?"

I felt a rush of emotion so intense it nearly took my breath away. A year ago, the idea of marriage would have sent me running for the hills. But now, standing here with Bennet, surrounded by the fruits of our labor and love, I couldn't imagine wanting anything else.

"Someday," I agreed, my voice barely above a whisper. "I think I'd like that very much."

Bennet's smile was radiant as he pulled me in for a kiss that felt like a promise, like a glimpse into a future filled with love and laughter and endless possibilities.

When we finally parted, both a little breathless, Bennet rested his forehead against mine. "So, partner, what's next on the agenda? World domination via wine and expertly planned events?"

I laughed, feeling lighter than I had in years. "Well, let's start with finalizing the plans for our New Year's Eve bash. Then maybe we can talk about that traveling wine festival idea. And after that..." I trailed off, my mind already racing with possibilities.

"After that, the sky's the limit," Bennet finished for me, his eyes shining with excitement and love.

As we cleaned up, working in perfect tandem as we had all evening, I couldn't help but feel a sense of anticipation for what the coming year would bring. There would be challenges, no doubt. Running a business with your partner wasn't always easy, and we still had plenty to learn about balancing our personal and professional lives.

But standing there in our beautiful new event space, the remnants of our successful first event around us, I knew that whatever came our way, Bennet and I would face it together. We'd built something special here - not just a business, but a partnership, a love story, a life.

And as I watched Bennet across the room, his sleeves rolled up as he tackled a stubborn wine stain on the table-cloth, I felt a surge of love so strong it almost overwhelmed me. This was home. This was where I belonged.

"Hey, Bennet?" I called out, unable to keep the smile from my voice.

He looked up, eyebrows raised in question. "Yeah?"

"I love you," I said simply. "Just thought you should know."

His answering smile was like the sun coming out from behind the clouds. "I love you too, Quinn. More than all the wine in this vineyard."

Have you read all the books in the Cozy Autumn Romance series?

# ABOUT ANN LAUREL

Ann loves writing about life and issues Christian couples face, all with a big dose of romance.

Sign up for Ann's newsletter.

Printed in Dunstable, United Kingdom